DATE DUE

16			
10			
APR 29 1999			
APR 17			
MAY 02			
MAY 11			

Mazer, Anne c.2

The salamander room

the Salamander Room

by ANNE MAZER
illustrated by STEVE JOHNSON

Alfred A. Knopf New York

THIS IS A BORZOI BOOK
PUBLISHED BY ALFRED A. KNOPF, INC.

 Published in the United States by Alfred A. Knopf, Inc., New York, and simultaneously in Canada by Random House of Canada Limited, Toronto. Distributed by Random House, Inc., New York.
Book design by Lou Fancher
Manufactured in Singapore

2 4 6 8 0 9 7 5 3 1

Library of Congress Cataloging-in-Publication Data
Mazer, Anne. The salamander room / by Anne Mazer:
illustrated by Steve Johnson. p. cm.
Summary: A young boy finds a salamander
and thinks of the many things he can do
to make a perfect home for it.
ISBN 0-394-82945-X (trade)
ISBN 0-394-92945-4 (lib. bdg.)
[1. Salamanders—Fiction. 2. Ecology—Fiction.]
I. Johnson, Steve, ill. II. Title.
PZ7.M47396Sal 1991 [E]—dc20
90-33301 CIP AC

For Mollie

A. M.

For Joel, Erin, Dale, and Tessa,
and a special thanks to Dave R.

S. J.

Brian found a salamander in the woods. It was a little orange salamander that crawled through the dried leaves of the forest floor.

The salamander was warm and cozy in the boy's hand. "Come live with me," Brian said.

He took the salamander home.

“Where will he sleep?” his mother asked.

“I will make him a salamander bed to sleep in. I will cover him with leaves that are fresh and green, and bring moss that looks like little stars to be a pillow for his head. I will bring crickets to sing him to sleep and bullfrogs to tell him good-night stories.”

"And when he wakes up, where will he play?"

"I will carpet my room with shiny wet leaves and water them so he can slide around and play.

I will bring tree stumps into
my room so he can climb up the bark
and sun himself on top. And I will bring
boulders that he can creep over."

"He will miss his friends in the forest."

"I will bring salamander friends to play with him."

"They will be hungry. How will you feed them?"

"I will bring insects to live in my room. And every day I will catch some and feed the salamanders. And I will make little pools of water on top of the boulders so they can drink whenever they are thirsty."

"The insects will multiply, and soon there will be bugs and insects everywhere."

"I will find birds to eat the extra bugs and insects. And the bullfrogs will eat them too."

"Where will the birds and bullfrogs live?"

"I will bring trees for the birds to roost in, and make ponds for the frogs."

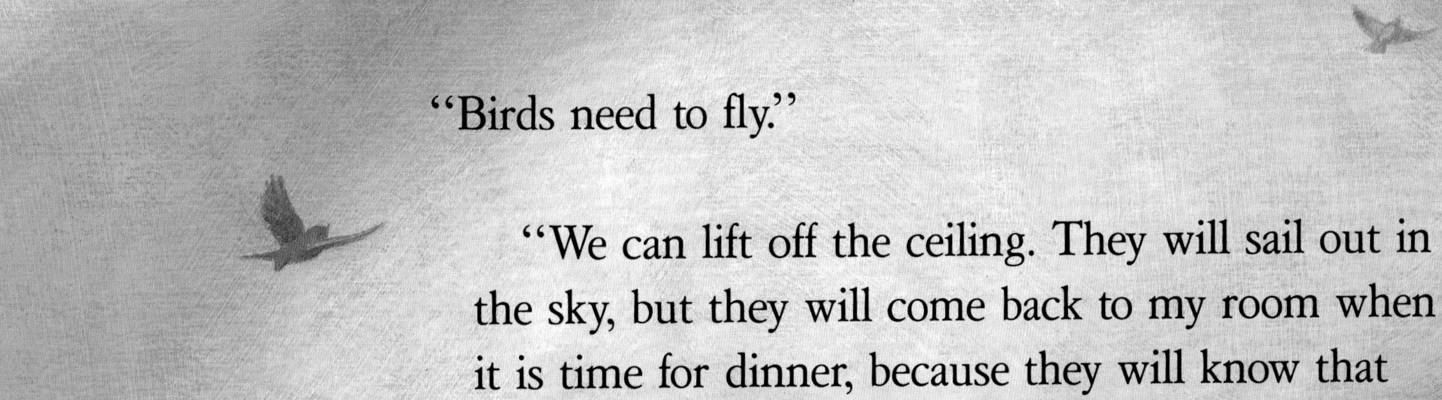

"Birds need to fly."

"We can lift off the ceiling. They will sail out in the sky, but they will come back to my room when it is time for dinner, because they will know that the biggest, juiciest insects are there."

"But the trees—how will they grow?"

"The rain will come through the open roof,
and the sun, too. And vines will
creep up the walls of my room,
and ferns will grow under my bed.
There will be big white mushrooms
and moss like little stars growing around
the tree stumps that the salamanders climb on."

"And you—
where will you sleep?"

"I will sleep on a bed under the stars, with the moon shining through the green leaves of the trees; owls will hoot and crickets will sing; and next to me, on the boulder with its head resting on soft moss, the salamander will sleep."